HELPING YOUR BRAND-NEW

Here's how to make first-time reading easy and fun:

▶ Read the introduction at the beginning of each story aloud. Look through the pictures together so that your child can see what happens in the story before reading the words.

▶ Read one or two pages to your child, placing your finger under each word.

▶ Let your child touch the words and read the rest of the story. Give him or her time to figure out each new word.

▶ If your child gets s... might say, *"Try som... picture. What woul...*

▶ If your child is still stuck, supply the right word. This will allow him or her to continue to read and enjoy the story. You might say, *"Could this word be 'ball'?"*

▶ Always praise your child. Praise what he or she reads correctly, and praise good tries too.

▶ Give your child lots of chances ...d the story again and again. ...our child reads, the more ...e or she will become.

First edition 2011

Library of Congress Cataloging-in-Publication Data is available.

Library of Congress Catalog Card Number pending

ISBN 978-0-7636-5067-4

10 11 12 13 14 15 SWT 10 9 8 7 6 5 4 3 2 1

Printed in Dongguan, Guangdong, China

This book was typeset in Arta Medium.
The illustrations were done digitally.

Candlewick Press
99 Dover Street
Somerville, Massachusetts 02144

visit us at www.candlewick.com

BIG BIRD
AT HOME

CANDLEWICK PRESS

ILLUSTRATED BY **Ernie Kwiat**

Contents

BIG BIRD CLEANS

Introduction

This story is called *Big Bird Cleans*. It's about how Big Bird and Abby put things away and sweep, mop, and dust. The room is clean, but Big Bird and Abby are dirty!

3

Big Bird puts away some blocks.

Abby puts away some books.

5

Big Bird sweeps the floor.

Abby mops the floor.

Big Bird folds his blanket.

Abby dusts the pictures.

The room is clean.

10

Big Bird and Abby are dirty!

BIG BIRD SHARES A SNACK

Introduction

This story is called *Big Bird Shares a Snack.* It's about how Big Bird and Abby set out plates, cups, muffins, and apples. Then the Count joins them for a snack.

Big Bird sets out three plates.

14

Abby sets out three cups.

Big Bird sets out three napkins.

16

Abby sets out three muffins.

17

Big Bird sets out three apples.

18

The Count knocks at the door.

The Count has three flowers.

20

The three friends share a snack!

BIG BIRD THE ARTIST

Introduction

This story is called *Big Bird the Artist*.
It's about how Big Bird and Oscar draw
a picture together. Big Bird draws happy
things, and Oscar draws grouchy things!

Big Bird draws a picture.

24

Oscar draws a picture.

Big Bird draws flowers.

26

Oscar draws garbage.

Big Bird draws the sun.

28

Oscar draws rain.

Big Bird draws an umbrella.

30

"I give up!" says Oscar.

BIG BIRD AND GROVER MOVE

Introduction

This story is called *Big Bird and Grover Move*. It's about how Big Bird and Grover move different parts of their bodies. Then they dance!

Grover shakes his head.

Big Bird waves his wings.

Grover kicks his leg.

Big Bird wiggles his tail.

Grover taps his feet.

38

Big Bird swings his beak.

Grover lifts his arms.

40

Grover and Big Bird dance!